D1454924

ISBN 978-1-84135-784-3

Adapted by Jane Carruth
Illustrated by Rene Cloke

This edition first published 2010

Published by Award Publications Limited,
The Old Riding School, The Welbeck Estate,
Worksop, Nottinghamshire, S80 3LR

10 1

Printed in China

The Wind in the Willows

By the River Bank

From Kenneth Grahame's
Classic Stories

Award Publications Limited

Mole had been very busy all morning spring cleaning his little house.

He had swept the floor with his big broom, dusted the table and chairs with his yellow duster and now he was whitewashing the walls of his burrow.

"Bother all this spring cleaning!" Mole said aloud. "I've had enough!"

And so he stopped working and bolted down the narrow dark tunnel that led into the fields above his little underground home.

"This is the life for me!" Mole cried, as he trotted through the sweet-scented grass. "All that dusting and cleaning is not good for a fellow's spirits!"

Mole felt so happy as he made his way along the side of the hedge that he sang a jolly song to himself and did a little dance.

It was a lovely day and Mole decided to stay away from home for as long as he could. He wandered through one meadow and then on to the next until – quite suddenly – he came upon a river.

Mole had never seen such a river before and he sat down on the grassy bank to gaze at it.

After a time he caught sight of a brown little face with whiskers, watching him from a dark hole in the opposite bank. Then the mysterious creature emerged from its hole. It was Ratty, the water rat!

"Hello, Mole!" called Ratty. "How would you like to pay me a visit? I'll come over and fetch you in my boat."

"I'd like that very much!" Mole called back.

Ratty wasted no time. He jumped into his boat and began rowing himself across the river. In only a few minutes he had reached the other side.

"I've never been in a boat before," Mole confessed as he climbed aboard. "But I'm quite sure I'll like it…"

"Then we'll make a day of it," Ratty said. "Let's have a picnic!"

Ratty rowed the boat back to his landing stage. He tied up and climbed into his hole. When he came out he was carrying a large, heavy picnic basket.

As soon as Ratty was sure Mole was quite comfortable, he took up the oars. "We'll make for the old watermill," he said, "even though that will mean that we'll have to row past the Wild Wood…"

"I've not heard of the Wild Wood before," Mole said, without much curiosity.

"That's just as well!" exclaimed Ratty. "The weasels and ferrets live there, and most of them are nothing but trouble!"

He said no more about the weasels, for he was busy steering his boat alongside the river bank so that they could find a spot to land and set out their picnic.

Ratty spread the picnic things on the grass opposite the water mill and as Mole watched him, he sighed a happy sigh!

There was so much to eat, Mole didn't know what to try first...

It was one of the best days of his life!

As they lay in the sun, Ratty and Mole talked about all the things they enjoyed most in the world and Mole began to feel that he had known Ratty all his life.

He was just about to say so when, without warning, a wet and furry head popped out of the water.

It was Otter!

"Well, I never!" cried Otter, climbing on to the bank. "What a greedy pair! You could have invited me to your picnic, Ratty!"

To Mole's amazement, Otter began helping himself to the rest of the food. Before Ratty could stop him, he'd gobbled up everything within reach.

When Otter saw there was nothing much left, he wiped his paws and whiskers.

"Everybody seems to be out on the river today," he remarked absentmindedly.

"We haven't seen anybody," Ratty said. "That is, apart from yourself, of course."

"Well, Toad is out for one. He's in his brand new boat and he's wearing some very smart boating clothes."

At that moment, Toad flashed into view, rowing as hard as he could. Ratty waved to him excitedly, but Toad just shook his head and rowed on up the river.

"I-I don't think I have had the pleasure of ever meeting Mr Toad," said Mole, somewhat shyly. "He seems to be a very important person."

"Well, *he* certainly thinks he is!" Ratty chuckled.

"If you ask me," said Otter loudly, "he's no more important than old Mother Rabbit over there on the far bank. Toad may have plenty of money, but she works all day long to gather food for her huge family."

Mole had never met Mr Toad or Mother Rabbit, so he didn't know what to think of it all.

Just then, Toad came back into view. He was clearly enjoying himself in his boat.

"It would be nice if you could meet Toad," Ratty said to Mole. And he scrambled to his feet and began waving frantically, making all kinds of signals to Toad to come ashore.

"I wouldn't waste your time," said Otter, as Toad rowed on with scarcely a backward glance towards the bank. "All he wants to do is to show off his new boat!"

Mole and Ratty were now beginning to feel very sleepy after their picnic, but not Otter. He was still hungry!

"I tell you what—" he began, and then broke off. He had seen a big fat mayfly and, with scarcely a ripple, he dived into the water after it.

"What a wonderful day this has been," sighed Mole, when Ratty at last said it was time for them to go home.

Mole helped Ratty pack away what was left of their picnic and they were soon on the river once more.

As they glided along, Mole suddenly cried with excitement, "Ratty! Ratty! Please let me row! I simply must try it!"

Before Ratty could reply, Mole jumped up and grabbed hold of the oars, knocking him backwards off his seat.

"Be careful!" Ratty shouted. "You'll have us both in the water!"

But it was too late. Into the river they both went with a mighty *SPLASH*!

Mole spluttered and choked as the water closed over his head. But Ratty was a fine swimmer and quickly came to his rescue, pulling him out on to the bank.

Then he dived into the water again to recover the little boat and fish up the picnic basket from the bottom of the river.

Mole was so ashamed of himself that all he could say was, "I'm so very sorry, Ratty. Can you ever forgive me?"

"Of course I can!" Ratty said cheerfully. "It was all rather fun, you know! Now be a good fellow and cheer up!"

Mole was so touched by Ratty's kind words that he brushed away a tear with his paw, which Ratty pretended not to notice.

"I tell you what," Ratty said at last. "Why don't you come home with me, Mole, and stay for a few days. I'll teach you how to swim and how to row and we'll have a jolly time together."

"There is absolutely nothing in the whole world I would like better," replied Mole, with great feeling.

"That's settled then," Ratty cried, as he helped Mole into the boat and took up the oars. "We'll be home soon and then you can dry yourself off properly."

As soon as they reached home, Ratty made a good fire in the parlour and insisted that Mole wore his best dressing gown to warm himself up. Then Ratty produced a very tasty supper for them both.

As he sat in front of the roaring fire with a mug of warm milky tea in his hand, Mole felt completely at home. He said as much to Ratty, who immediately set about making plans for the next day's adventure.

"What do you say we go to Toad Hall," he suggested, "and visit Mr Toad?"

"What a splendid idea!" Mole exclaimed. "I would love to meet Mr Toad and see Toad Hall for myself!"

"And so you shall," said Ratty smiling. "You won't be disappointed, I'm sure," he went on, "for it's the grandest house for miles around and very big indeed."

"I-I do hope I won't be too ordinary for your Mr Toad," Mole said shyly.

"Of course you won't," Ratty declared. "We'll set out first thing in the morning."

After more talk about Toad Hall, Ratty showed Mole to the spare room and wished him a good night's sleep. "Don't forget," he said, "you are welcome to stay here for as long as you like."

They set out early the next morning by boat. After Ratty had been rowing for some time he said, "You'll see Toad Hall round the next bend in the river."

As the large, handsome brick house came into view, Mole was quite overcome at the sight. "My, my!" he kept saying.

Ratty smiled to himself as he steered his boat to Toad's landing stage and tied it fast. Then he helped Mole to step ashore.

The smooth green lawns ran right down to the water's edge and presently Ratty and Mole found themselves strolling along between banks of bright flowers.

"Look, there he is!" Ratty cried suddenly.
"There is Toad himself!"

Toad was sitting in a wicker chair when
he caught sight of the two friends and he
dropped the large map he was studying and
bellowed, "Hooray! How splendid! I was
just going to send for you, Ratty!"

"Calm down, Toad. Here I am," said
Ratty. "And this is my friend Mole, who has
come to visit you."

"Why, I'll need you both," Toad said
eagerly. "You are the very animals I want to
see!"

"Is it about rowing?" Ratty asked.

"Just come and see!" cried Toad.

Toad took the two friends into the stable yard and there – shining new, and painted bright yellow and green with red wheels – stood a splendid wooden caravan!

"Well," said Toad, trying hard not to look too pleased with himself. "Who doesn't yearn for life on the open road? This is the finest caravan ever built – and it belongs to me!"

Mole had never seen anything so grand in his life, and he said so, for which Toad loved him all the more!

"Come inside, my dear fellow," Toad said. "And you too, Ratty."

"I'll stay on the step, if it's all the same to you," Ratty said, and it was clear to Mole that he was not very impressed at all.

"Look," gestured Toad, ignoring Ratty. "It's quite complete for a long journey, with all the provisions you could possibly want!"

"It's wonderful, just wonderful!" Mole said, over and over again.

Ratty said nothing as Toad invited Mole to inspect the shelves and lockers, all crammed with tins and bottles, and jars of delicious jams and pickles.

"My goodness!" said Mole, now more impressed than ever.

"I've planned everything!" Toad cried. "We could set off this very day. What do you say?"

"I say – rubbish!" said Ratty from the step outside. "Absolute rubbish!"

"Please, Ratty," Toad pleaded. "Do say yes! I just can't manage without you and it will be such a splendid adventure."

Ratty looked at Mole and saw at once that he was longing to go. And so, at last, he agreed. "Oh, very well – but don't blame me if things turn out badly."

In no time at all, Toad had harnessed the old grey horse he kept in the field and they were off!

Toad felt like a king as friendly walkers stopped to admire his outfit, and rabbits sat up on their hind legs to watch them pass.

And how pleasant it was when night fell, to stop and have supper sitting on the grass by the side of the caravan.

Alas, trouble was not far away. The very next day they were rolling gently along the high road, with Mole leading the horse, when all at once there came a very loud POOP-POOP behind them.

A magnificent shining motor car rushed past, enveloping them in a cloud of choking dust. The horse bucked and reared and Mole was dragged off his feet. Toad finished up sitting in the road, and the caravan landed in the ditch.

The caravan was a complete wreck, and the three friends had a long and weary walk to the nearest town to catch the train home. Ratty was so furious with Toad that he wouldn't speak to him. But Toad didn't seem to mind. All the way home he could talk about nothing but the shining motor car.

Mole couldn't help feeling sorry for Toad and said so to Ratty when they went out for a spot of fishing the next day. "You needn't bother yourself about Toad," Ratty replied. "I got word this morning – Toad has just ordered himself a very big and expensive, luxury motor car!"